For my three favorite poems:
Sadie, Lydia & Gabriel
& with endless gratitude to
Sheila, Nan & Cindy
SB

For Allie, Tyler, Scarlett
and Genevieve (my nieces
and nephew)
CD

Text copyright © 2019 by Shannon Bramer
Illustrations copyright © 2019 by Cindy Derby
Published in Canada and the USA in 2019 by Groundwood Books

Groundwood Books / House of Anansi Press
groundwoodbooks.com

We gratefully acknowledge for their financial support of our publishing
program the Canada Council for the Arts, the Ontario Arts Council and
the Government of Canada.

Canada Council **Conseil des Arts**
for the Arts du Canada

ONTARIO ARTS COUNCIL
CONSEIL DES ARTS DE L'ONTARIO
an Ontario government agency
un organisme du gouvernement de l'Ontario

With the participation of the Government of Canada
Avec la participation du gouvernement du Canada | Canadä

Library and Archives Canada Cataloguing in Publication
Bramer, Shannon, author
Climbing shadows : poems for children / Shannon Bramer ; illustrated
by Cindy Derby.
Issued in print and electronic formats.
ISBN 978-1-77306-095-8 (hardcover). — ISBN 978-1-77306-096-5 (PDF)
I. Derby, Cindy, illustrator II. Title.
PS8553.R269C55 2019   jC811'.54   C2018-903735-0
C2018-903736-9

The illustrations were done in watercolor, India ink and digital collage.
Design by Michael Solomon
Printed and bound in Malaysia

CLIMBING SHADOWS

POEMS FOR CHILDREN

PICTURES BY

SHANNON BRAMER   CINDY DERBY

GROUNDWOOD BOOKS
HOUSE OF ANANSI PRESS
TORONTO   BERKELEY

 Table of

Contents

Little Yellow House

Poem

lives

inside

a little

yellow

house.

Come

visit

her

with me?

I Love to Draw

A drawing is a poem
with a house in it
or a circle or a fox.
A drawing is a string
of letters I am practicing
and also stars I know
how to fit in all over
this sky. And when I
draw it's like driving
a fast car. There is a road
that bends and there is
wind in my hand and
I see things in my head
come loose on the
paper and there are my
eyes here, and my names
and my trees and faces
and crazy squiggles
and also this is a drawing
of my family because I
usually draw what I miss
or what I love. If you want
I will draw something
for you.

9

Skeleton Song

I'm not afraid of skeletons
Are you afraid of skeletons?

Skeletons are bones in the shape of a body
Are you afraid of bones in the shape of a body?

Sometimes the bones rattle
Bones rattle when skeletons dance

But I imagine a funny little smile
on the skeleton's face

I hear the crunchy, spiny, tinkling
music of cracking bones

And it makes me want to dance!

So you can only be afraid of skeletons
if you are afraid of your own bones

dancing

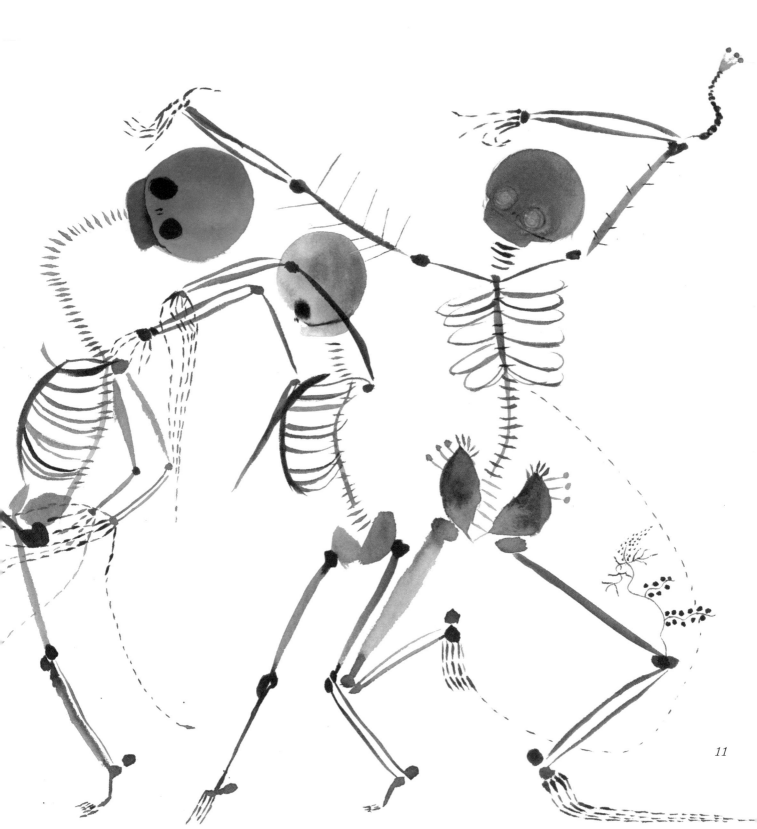

11

a spider way of thinking

i've got a spider way of thinking

    i live in light

        switches   broken fixtures

            dusty crystal chandeliers that sparkle on me

       and my tiny shadow   please

       let me make you something intricate

the world i love is on the ceiling

    in the tiny crack of window pane

moonlight

       where i am making you a new home   see

          my arms are my legs are my arms

silk ink lines

     calligraphy

i have a spider way of dreaming

        i drop so much thread

            and fly

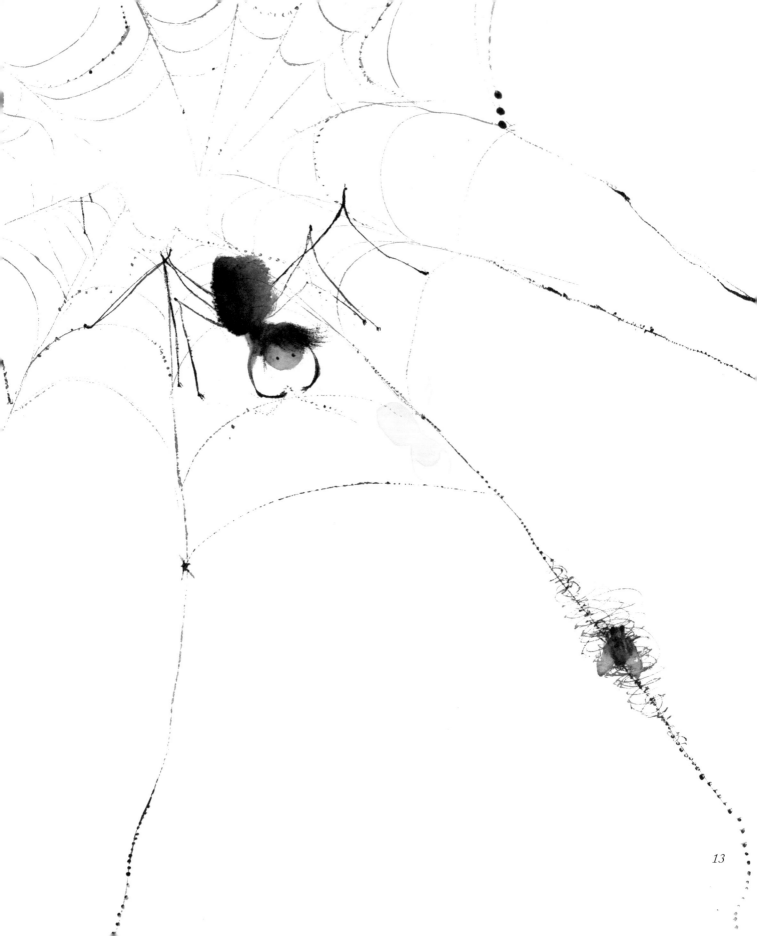

13

Three Hearts and No Bones at All

Did you know that octopuses have three hearts?
They can make themselves very small and slide away
from harm. They have three hearts and no bones at all
blocking their way out — like light coming in
under a door, octopuses can do that.
Octopuses love what people lose.
They collect keys, shells, jewels and broken
watches that have fallen to the bottom of the ocean.
You can't trap them. They are artists of escape.
Octopuses dream of climbing trees. They want
to climb trees more than anything else in the world
and if they did climb a tree they would know
what the tree tasted like because they taste everything
they touch and they see with their skin.
It's because of the three hearts, I think.
It's because of the three hearts that an octopus
in a tree becomes color all around her.

polka-dot song

polka dot   polka dot

you are not at all what i thought

i catch the sky in this tin pot

the sound of rain is polka dots

one alone is just a dot

but lots and lots are polka dots

i love to wear my polka dots

on hats and scarves   boots and socks

oh here's a dress that has a lot

of perfect purple polka dots

i hear a song in the circle i caught

you can't bump together

two polka dots

don't forget   i love you

when you feel a lot

my   darling   little   polka   dots

afterschool

i'm going to go home and tell my dad

today was hard   it was so hard

i don't want to go anymore

i want

    to be a puddle

I Don't Need a Poem

My hands are cold —
I lost my mittens
And I love my family
And my brother

I speak Romania
I like Canada

I can't go home, so

I am going to give my teacher
a flower tomorrow
I am going to give everyone
something from me

It's okay —
I don't need a poem
I am going to give
something to you

You Speak Violets

sometimes you are   quiet as a trillium   yet your eyes speak

the language of wild basil   red butterflies   impatient

for a buzzing loud summer   you've got a young forest inside you

i see waterfalls beyond tall   white   sleeping trees

birches   poplars   where everything is moving and alive

i see rushing water in your eyes when you get a new idea

sun through the branches making shadows inside you

when you find it hard   to say what you are feeling

you speak violets

My Cars Never Sleep

My two best cars are Crashout and Powerdog

Crashout is all business when he races

Powerdog thinks he can win his older brother's heart

and make him turn off the TV forever

They race in parking lots when the stores are closed

and all the windows are lit up with light

They race on roads of country when we go to Saskatchewan

to see my stepsisters and the sun setting

beyond the Cypress Hills

They race hard in the dirt and get white mud in the wheels!

My cars never sleep like me

They keep driving in my dreams

They want to race to the sun alone

So I have to let my cars really move and travel —

I have to let my best cars go even faster

and fly away from me like dragons

Penelope's Birthday

On Tuesday, it was Penelope's birthday

The sun hid in the clouds, too shy
to come to the party

There was a rusty old truck
full of balloons

Penelope got to open
the heavy blue doors

and set them all free

As soon as it was time for raspberry cake
it started to rain

Everyone was worried Penelope might cry —

But she didn't! She didn't!

Next year, Penelope wants her birthday
to be on Tuesday again

I hope I'm still her friend

Owl Secrets

I love an owl with eyes
that see to the bottom of me.
I am an ocean, I whisper to my owl.
I am old inside my body.
Because I know the secrets of owls,
I close my eyes and she opens hers.
Her wings fold over my sleep,
and her heart beats
through her feathers
so I can listen.

Owls love the dark,
like me   like you
                    you

Climbing Shadows

I have a kitten
in my night bedroom

See her tiny paws, ginger fur
tumbling along

bubbles of light
in the dark house I sleep in?

It's not ghosts —

It's only cars going by outside
making ribbons
on my walls and my kitten

is climbing shadows

The Envelope

My mommy is an envelope
an antelope   an artichoke
a fine porcupine

My mommy is a kitty
with a coffee   yawning
in her swivel chair

My mommy is a pearl
My mommy is a bear

My mommy is a blanket   a table
a castle   a shadow

My mommy is an avalanche
a big heavy love

My mommy is a sink   a pink
umbrella   a mitten
and a stove

My mommy is a lamp
a shell
a bed
a fat bouncy ball

My mommy is a bowl!

My mommy is a towel   My mommy
is a tree   My mommy is an envelope
with love inside for me

My mommy is a pillow
My mommy is a poem

My mommy is my mommy
My mommy is alone

My mommy is a nest
My mommy is a home

When She Grows Up

One house overlooking the ocean

Two cats called Persephone and Lorca

Three bowls of cherries for breakfast

Four purple orchids in the west window

Five quilts covered in roses

Six sandcastles in progress

Seven mature trees to climb with her children

Eight red dresses in the closet

Nine trips to Paris and counting

Ten wild island horses, running free alongside her

Dreaming Upside Down

The little brown bats
in my attic
sleep all day

dream

upside

down

Baby bat dreams of his mother
Mama bat dreams of her baby

    It's the same dream —
  They are flying

       together
           along cracking walls of sky
broken black echoes

      of buildings
         in shadows

      until they smell
        rocks   trees
water

    They taste wind   rain

  and have no words

      for where they must go

The Snow Is Melting

The sun is shining and the snow is melting
on Valentine's Day

My mom is pushing the stroller
through slush and broken ice
and there's lots of cold water shining
on the street

My baby brother is crying
because he won't put on his mittens
and it's hard getting up
this slippery hill

We're having a party and I made a valentine
for everyone in my class, even the boy
who called me stupid

You haven't got a mean bone in your body
is what my grumpy sister said about that

I'll probably save her a chocolate cupcake
I'll probably give her all my cinnamon hearts

Darkness Looks Like My Mom

She's in a long black dress. She kisses me
goodnight and reminds me how much she loves
rain and puddles, the deep dark puddles you jump
in when you dream. Her purse has a red silk
lining. She's got her keys in there when she goes out.
Darkness walks like a question mark out into
the moonlight and sometimes our cat follows her
all the way down the street because he hates
to see her go.

Eleanor's Poem

This poem doesn't like wearing shoes,
just like Eleanor.

This poem would rather eat the cookie before the carrot,
just like Eleanor.

This poem has had a sore throat all week,
just like Eleanor.

This poem is tired of wearing a pink snowsuit,
just like Eleanor.

This poem will not sit on the carpet,
and Eleanor won't either.

This poem is funny and determined
(to make you smile),
just like Eleanor.

A Question for Choying

Are you going to write it down?

You should because your words

are snowy animals in the woods.

Your letters are delicate like your hands.

This is my winter alphabet.

You are my snow angel on the carpet,

writing in your notebook.

Are you going to write it down?

You should because sometimes

the poem inside

disappears like a snowflake —

a tiny crystal star

in your shiny black hair

that melts away

nearly before it is seen.

  Christopher Iain Max Clyde Lauren Celine RUBY

 Finley

 JACK

Author's Note

The poems in *Climbing Shadows* originated in a kindergarten classroom at a public school in Toronto, where I worked as a lunchroom supervisor.

Being a lunchroom supervisor in a kindergarten room involves container opening, orange peeling, snowsuit detangling and mitten hunting. It is a social time for the students, where tender and hilarious conversations abound. Within a few weeks of my working in the school we all got to know each other, and the students, aged four and five, learned that I was a writer. I explained to them that when I wasn't in the classroom helping them with their containers, mittens and zippers, I was at home at my desk trying my best to create beautiful sentences, that I loved arranging words on paper like the pieces of a puzzle — that I was a poet.

Most of the kids found this information both mystifying and downright hilarious. Their incredulity made me feel passionate about sharing poetry with them, and with the enthusiastic support of a wonderful teacher, I began the routine of reading poems every Friday, in the tiny window of time they had before going outside.

I shared the work of writers ranging from Emily Dickinson to Federico García Lorca to Gwendolyn Brooks. I brought in illustrated books of poetry for them to browse through; I wanted them to see all the different ways a poem could look on the page. I wanted them to hear all the different ways a poem could sound. I read Dennis Lee and Gwendolyn MacEwen. I read Joy Harjo. Sometimes I read my own poems, because a poet doesn't have to be someone fancy or special — a poet could be a mom. A poet could be a kindergarten lunchroom supervisor who thinks the word *crunchy* is as powerful as the word *broccoli* is beautiful.

My kindies learned that poetry could make them feel and see and remember things. A poem could tell a sad story or it could make them laugh; it could make them think. A poem could be hard to understand and beautiful to listen to at the same time. They learned that a poem could be about anything — a favorite toy car, a video game, a kitten, a new baby brother. Even a fictional character from a favorite movie could become the subject of a poem.

I offered to write them each a poem about anything they wanted for Valentine's Day. They said, I want my poem to be about a princess; I want my poem to be about my mom; I want mine to be about ninjas! I made a Valentine's Day anthology and gave them each a copy, and for weeks afterwards that was what we read together on "Poetry Fridays." Meanwhile, the anthologies were traveling home to be read with their parents. Many of those valentine poems appear in this book.

After creating that anthology, with a single poem in mind for each child in the class, the idea of writing poetry for children took hold of me. My kindies' stories and observations, our conversations and friendship made these poems possible. *Climbing Shadows: Poems for Children* is the result of the wonderful exchange between myself, poetry and children who needed me for a little more than an hour at lunchtime — when we had just enough time to eat a sandwich and more than enough time to read a poem.

 Lilly

 Davis

 Izzy

 GRACE

 Cohen

 LoGAN

Jackson

 Beatrice

Antonio

 44 Amy Graham Emilio Maitri Loenne Annabelle

Bella

Piper